BOSTON
Tea Party

BOSTON
Tea Party

by PAMELA DUNCAN EDWARDS

illustrations by HENRY COLE

PUFFIN BOOKS

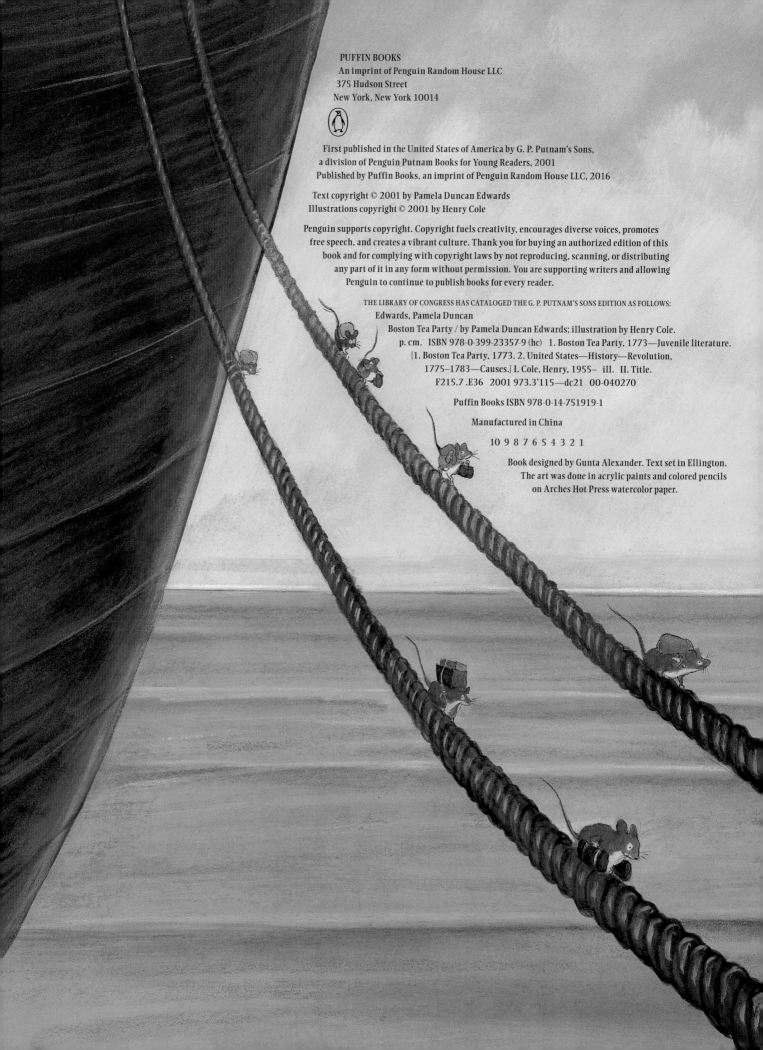

PUFFIN BOOKS
An imprint of Penguin Random House LLC
375 Hudson Street
New York, New York 10014

First published in the United States of America by G. P. Putnam's Sons,
a division of Penguin Putnam Books for Young Readers, 2001
Published by Puffin Books, an imprint of Penguin Random House LLC, 2016

THE LIBRARY OF CONGRESS HAS CATALOGED THE G. P. PUTNAM'S SONS EDITION AS FOLLOWS:
Edwards, Pamela Duncan
Boston Tea Party / by Pamela Duncan Edwards; illustration by Henry Cole.
p. cm. ISBN 978-0-399-23357-9 (hc) 1. Boston Tea Party, 1773—Juvenile literature.
[1. Boston Tea Party, 1773. 2. United States—History—Revolution,
1775–1783—Causes.] I. Cole, Henry, 1955– ill. II. Title.
F215.7 .E36 2001 973.3'115—dc21 00-040270

Puffin Books ISBN 978-0-14-751919-1

Manufactured in China

10 9 8 7 6 5 4 3 2 1

Book designed by Gunta Alexander. Text set in Ellington.
The art was done in acrylic paints and colored pencils
on Arches Hot Press watercolor paper.

To Janie West, a devoted teacher — P. D. E.

For Roberta, my cup of tea! With love — Hen

These are the leaves that grew on a bush in a far-off land and became part of the Boston Tea Party.

Only pick the new shoots. They're the ones that get sent to the factory to be made into tea.

My Uncle Bert is a great traveler. He says tea grows in places other than India, like China and Africa.

This is the tea that was made from the leaves
that grew on a bush in a far-off land
and became part of the Boston Tea Party.

This is the king on his English throne
who declared, "Tax the tea!"
that was made from the leaves
that grew on a bush in a far-off land
and became part of the Boston Tea Party.

These are the colonists who cried, "No!"
to the king on his English throne who declared,
"Tax the tea!" that was made from the leaves
that grew on a bush in a far-off land
and became part of the Boston Tea Party.

This is the cargo being carried in ships to the shores
of the colonists who cried, "No!"
to the king on his English throne who declared,
"Tax the tea!" that was made from the leaves
that grew on a bush in a far-off land
and became part of the Boston Tea Party.

These are the patriots who made plans to dump the cargo
being carried in ships to the shores
of the colonists who cried, "No!"
to the king on his English throne who declared,
"Tax the tea!" that was made from the leaves
that grew on a bush in a far-off land
and became part of the Boston Tea Party.

Sam and John Adams have called a meeting. Paul Revere, Joseph Warren and John Hancock are all here.

Hurrah! The Sons of Liberty will know what to do.

Did they have cheese for supper?

These are the disguises worn by the patriots
who made plans to dump the cargo
being carried in ships to the shores
of the colonists who cried, "No!"
to the king on his English throne who declared,
"Tax the tea!" that was made from the leaves
that grew on a bush in a far-off land
and became part of the Boston Tea Party.

These are the sailors scared by disguises worn by the patriots
who made plans to dump the cargo
being carried in ships to the shores
of the colonists who cried, "No!"
to the king on his English throne who declared,
"Tax the tea!" that was made from the leaves
that grew on a bush in a far-off land
and became part of the Boston Tea Party.

This is the harbor stained dark brown. "Like a giant teapot!"
shouted the sailors scared by disguises worn by the patriots
who made plans to dump the cargo
being carried in ships to the shores
of the colonists who cried, "No!"
to the king on his English throne who declared,
"Tax the tea!" that was made from the leaves
that grew on a bush in a far-off land
and became part of the Boston Tea Party.

These are tea chests, 340 in number, which bobbed in the harbor
stained dark brown. "Like a giant teapot!"
shouted the sailors scared by disguises worn by the patriots
who made plans to dump the cargo
being carried in ships to the shores
of the colonists who cried, "No!"
to the king on his English throne who declared,
"Tax the tea!" that was made from the leaves
that grew on a bush in a far-off land
and became part of the Boston Tea Party.

These are the soldiers who fought for freedom
remembering the tea chests, 340 in number, which bobbed in the harbor
stained dark brown. "Like a giant teapot!"
shouted the sailors scared by disguises worn by the patriots
who made plans to dump the cargo
being carried in ships to the shores
of the colonists who cried, "No!"
to the king on his English throne who declared,
"Tax the tea!" that was made from the leaves
that grew on a bush in a far-off land
and became part of the Boston Tea Party.

The redcoats are coming!

We're ready for them.

These are Americans, independent and free,
who honor the soldiers who fought for freedom
remembering the tea chests, 340 in number, which bobbed in the harbor
stained dark brown. "Like a giant teapot!"
shouted the sailors scared by disguises worn by the patriots
who made plans to dump the cargo
being carried in ships to the shores
of the colonists who cried, "No!"
to the king on his English throne who declared,
"Tax the tea!" that was made from the leaves
that grew on a bush in a far-off land
and became part of THE BOSTON TEA PARTY.

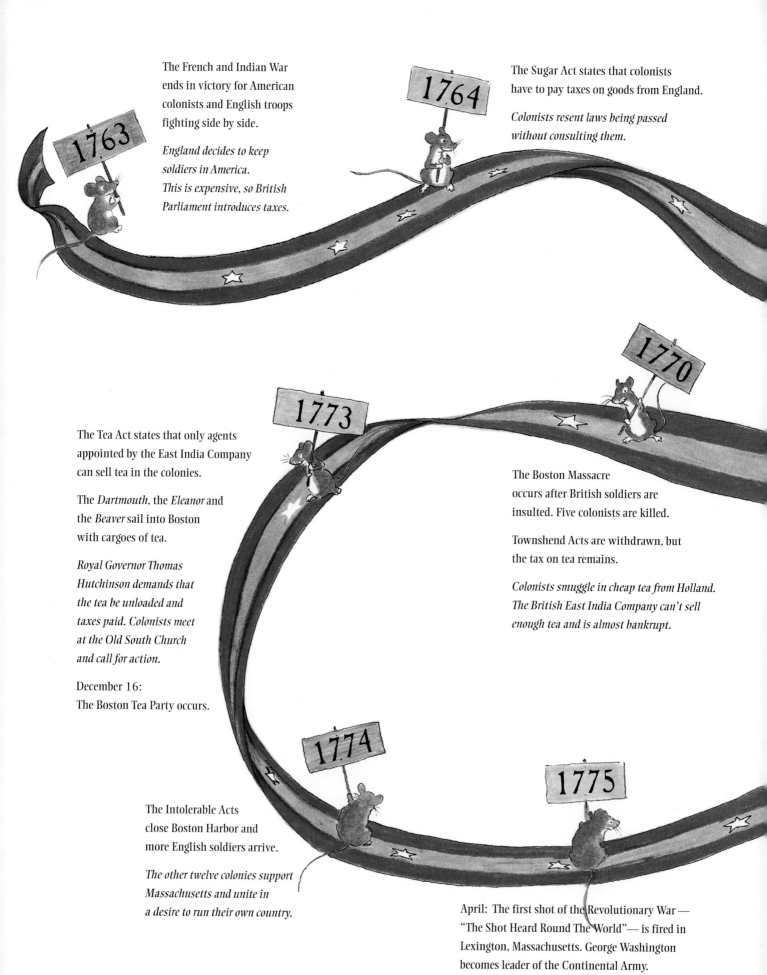

1763

The French and Indian War ends in victory for American colonists and English troops fighting side by side.

England decides to keep soldiers in America. This is expensive, so British Parliament introduces taxes.

1764

The Sugar Act states that colonists have to pay taxes on goods from England.

Colonists resent laws being passed without consulting them.

1770

The Boston Massacre occurs after British soldiers are insulted. Five colonists are killed.

Townshend Acts are withdrawn, but the tax on tea remains.

Colonists smuggle in cheap tea from Holland. The British East India Company can't sell enough tea and is almost bankrupt.

1773

The Tea Act states that only agents appointed by the East India Company can sell tea in the colonies.

The *Dartmouth*, the *Eleanor* and the *Beaver* sail into Boston with cargoes of tea.

Royal Governor Thomas Hutchinson demands that the tea be unloaded and taxes paid. Colonists meet at the Old South Church and call for action.

December 16:
The Boston Tea Party occurs.

1774

The Intolerable Acts close Boston Harbor and more English soldiers arrive.

The other twelve colonies support Massachusetts and unite in a desire to run their own country.

1775

April: The first shot of the Revolutionary War — "The Shot Heard Round The World"— is fired in Lexington, Massachusetts. George Washington becomes leader of the Continental Army.

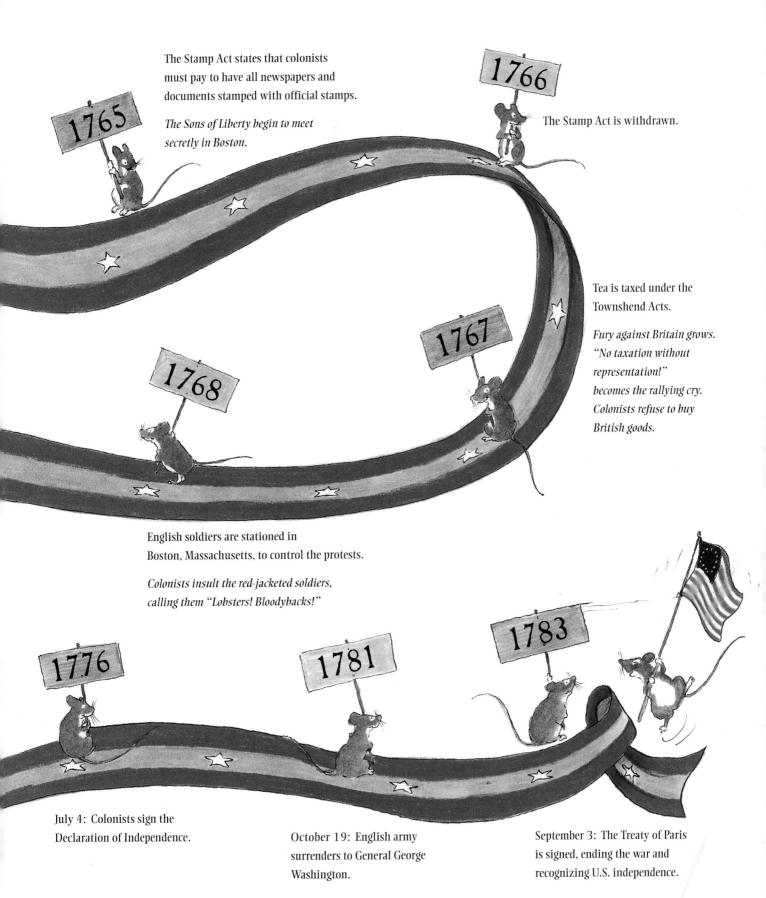

The Stamp Act states that colonists must pay to have all newspapers and documents stamped with official stamps.

The Sons of Liberty begin to meet secretly in Boston.

1765

1766

The Stamp Act is withdrawn.

Tea is taxed under the Townshend Acts.

Fury against Britain grows. "No taxation without representation!" becomes the rallying cry. Colonists refuse to buy British goods.

1767

1768

English soldiers are stationed in Boston, Massachusetts, to control the protests.

Colonists insult the red-jacketed soldiers, calling them "Lobsters! Bloodybacks!"

1776

1781

1783

July 4: Colonists sign the Declaration of Independence.

October 19: English army surrenders to General George Washington.

September 3: The Treaty of Paris is signed, ending the war and recognizing U.S. independence.